T0380736

THE MYTHICAL JOURNEY OF THE DRAGON SISTERS

A fairy tale for children of all ages

Ur-Adorabelle

Balboa Press books may be ordered through booksellers or by contacting:

Balboa Press
A Division of Hay House
1663 Liberty Drive
Bloomington, IN 47403
www.balboapress.com
844-682-1282

ISBN: 978-1-9822-1688-7 (sc)
ISBN: 978-1-9822-1689-4 (e)

Library of Congress Control Number: 2020920051

Print information available on the last page.

Balboa Press rev. date: 08/22/2022

BALBOA.PRESS
A DIVISION OF HAY HOUSE

CONTENTS

Chapter 1

The Beginning

Many, many, many moons ago, when there was no such thing as time or people as we know today, there was just Father Sky and Mother Earth. Some say that Father existed first as the Galaxy, however, some claim that their unseen observation about Mother was the fact she quietly calculated that perfect moment, like a spark waiting to explode, also known as The Big Bang. But it doesn't really matter at all who was first, because it is irrelevant to this story that started before time existed.

Loving days of warm sunshine and tender nights of twinkling stars shined upon Mother Earth ever so brightly, but she felt something was missing. So she consulted with Father Sky about using their combined creativity and the idea of birthing something amazing. At that time the only presence on Mother was the Rock and Plant Beings and the Fair Folk. The Fair Folk made their homes either in the majestic rolling hills of green vegetation, massive formations of extraordinary rocks or the large bodies of crystalline water that covered more than half of Mother Earth.

Father Sky stated he wanted an extremely strong courageous creature that possessed the talents to fly, swim, walk or crawl and breathe out fire if needed. Mother Earth thought this creature would be extra special as it would embody all the elements in its being so she agreed to Father's idea of creation. Mother chose the color of a shimmering midnight blue. Mother also designed the shape of this creature with a huge head with what would appear to be horns, whiskers or a beard of sorts and a long strong neck with an elongated snout shared with a rather big mouth that housed a forked tongue and large sharp ivory teeth. It would have enormous eyes that could see amazingly far and keen hearing built into the sides of its head. And the creature's body design would be very muscular with impenetrable scales that almost had the appearance of iridescent feathers at times, along with a thick tail that would assist it with power and balance. She designed the limbs to be short and massive with gigantic wings which would tuck away nicely under its huge shoulder blades. Father gleefully added the ability to retain the breath of fire and release smoke from its nostrils.

As Father and Mother were sharing their creative birthing ideas with each other, the creature was forming inside a colossal purplish egg. And so it was hatched and Mother named this creature Coal. She called it a Dragon.

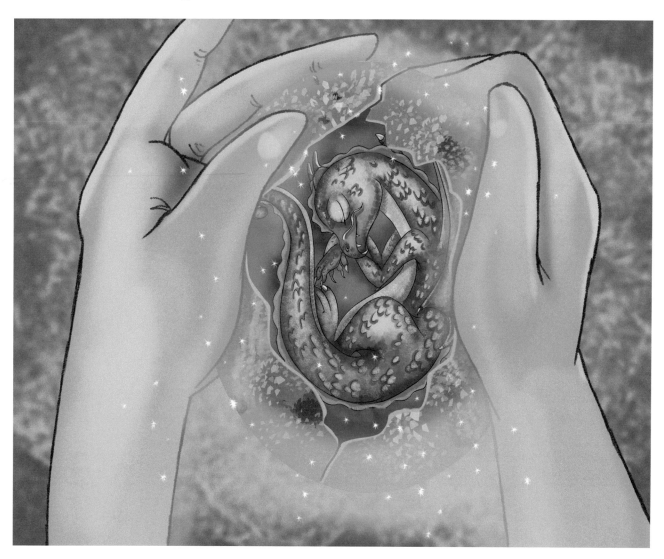

Coal was very curious about everything and followed the Fair Folk around without giving them a moments rest. At first, the Fair Folk found this Dragon creature, Coal, to be very cute and endearing, especially the Fairies who loved to ride on the wings of the Dragon.

It was a joy ride for sure as they giggled and laughed and had so much fun with Coal. And it was a breathtaking site to see as the Fairies lit up the wings of Coal with a rainbow of colors, and they called this display the twinkling of twilight.

Each Fairy had its own unique color and had the ability to grow in size but preferred to stay tiny. They were considered the flashiest of all the Fair Folk. Because they moved so fast, they would leave streams of colors everywhere they went, and they were the ones responsible for decorating the wide array of beautifully colored flowers. Eventually the Fairies made their homes in amongst the flowers.

However, after thousands, maybe millions, of years most of the Fair Folk grew tired of Coal as she was preventing them from their passion of taking care of nature. Coal's innocently bad behavior like stepping on freshly planted flowers, burning the brush with its breath of fire, dislodging stones and crystals, as well as disturbing the ocean by causing the waves to flow against the currents created havoc with most of the Fair Folks way of life.

Her bad manners were getting on most everyone's nerves as she was unknowingly disrupting everyone's life in some way, shape or form.

So the Fair Folk formed a committee and secretly called a meeting but needed to meet without Coal around.

So the Brownies, Dyrads, Elves, Fairies, Fire Spirits, Gnomes, Kobolds, Leprechauns, Limoniades, Mer-People, Nixies, Nymphs, Pixies, Selkies, Sylphs, Trolls, Undines, and Water Sprites all got together under the great rock that was nestled into the great hill by the great sea during the time of day the Dragon was napping. The crashing waves of the sea prevented the Dragon from hearing what they were planning.

After much deliberation they decided to approach Mother Earth to seek a solution with her. Because they loved Coal so much, the Fairies bravely offered to go to talk with Mother Earth. Mother Earth lovingly created all beings and she's a powerful force who must be respected.

To show their honor and love for their Mother Earth they did a ritual of gratitude and presented her with the most beautiful heart shaped golden leaf covered with fresh dew that glistened in the sunlight. Mother appreciated their honoring of her and listened thoughtfully to their dilemma.

It was obvious that things needed to change, and Mother decided that Coal needed someone of her stature as a playmate.

Chapter 2

The Birth of the Sister Dragon

ight away Mother Earth called on Father Sky to help with the creation of another Dragon. They used the same model type but slightly smaller than Coal and added peace, patience, discernment, grace, love and wisdom to the mix, as well as the ability to breathe out either fire or water. They also included fins that attached just under the pits of its limbs, as well as webbed feet for the ability to swim incredibly well and gills to breathe under water if needed. The color of this Dragon would be a very light iridescent greenish blue and so it was named Aqua.

Another major difference between the two Dragons is that Coal has oil running through her veins just like blood and Aqua has saltwater running through her veins with oil only in her liver. Because they have oil in their bodies, they are able to breathe out fire. They are purely organic, however toxic, particularly Coal, and especially if she was injured or killed for any reason.

Aqua and Coal became the best of friends - Sister Dragons. They were inseparable and communicated with each other by using different vocal tones from purring to squealing or howling to roaring and even snorting. Aqua learned quickly to put out any fires Coal started and how to cool Coal down if she became hot-headed. They frolicked on the land creating mountains out of hills and valleys out of flatlands. Aqua was an amazing swimmer and moved the sea around creating lakes, rivers, streams and brooks. It has been said that Aqua created the salt in the sea when one day she cried because she lost sight of her sister when they were swimming together in the great waters.

Aqua was very sensitive and sentimental. She loved her sister Coal, and found no fault or burden in her, only unconditional love. The only thing Coal could do better than Aqua was create a bigger fire with more smoke. But Aqua knew that water had a great advantage over fire and that was to snuff it out. So, the Fair Folk smartly observed that water is more powerful than fire.

The Fair Folk were delighted with the presence of Aqua in their lives. Twice a year they celebrated each Dragon with a big festival. Everyone joined in by singing, dancing, making music and storytelling. They all liked a good time. However not a creature ate or drank a thing, they lived solely off the essence of nature. Smelling the sweet aroma of the blossoms and absorbing the beauty of life in their hearts. That's how they survived.

The Fair Folk were nurturers and caretakers of these lovely objects of beauty. Brilliant sparkling crystals and lush green landscapes were painted with a variety of beauteous flowers, surrounded by the magick of the glistening deep blue sea. They walked in beauty always. And they were ever so grateful for this golden opportunity. One might say that it was truly paradise.

Chapter 3

A Galaxy Shift

After many years of living in paradise, Father Sky consulted Mother Earth about an event that was on the rise due to shifts in the galaxy. It was to become known as the first Ice Age. Father requested that Mother would handle all the creatures living on Earth and forewarn them of this potential dilemma. Joining together, all the Fair Folk, especially the Gnomes, worked extremely hard and fast to build underground tunnels that lead to the other side of the planet. Mother took her Dragon children aside and told them a story about the great shift of the planet and explained how cold it was going to get on planet earth. Neither Dragon liked the idea of ice cold and said they could melt it with their fire breathing abilities. Mother explained that it would go on for millions of years and even they could not keep up with this shift in the weather. Her solution was to invite them into her bosom and keep them safe and warm as they sleep peacefully. They agreed and Coal proceeded to travel to the center of Mother Earth and Aqua to the bottom of the deepest sea. For billions of years they lay resting in their safe places. However, every now and then they toss and turn and disturb nature a bit with an eruption of volcanoes, earthquakes, tidal waves and hurricanes. These occurrences are all just a natural reaction to their movement underground.

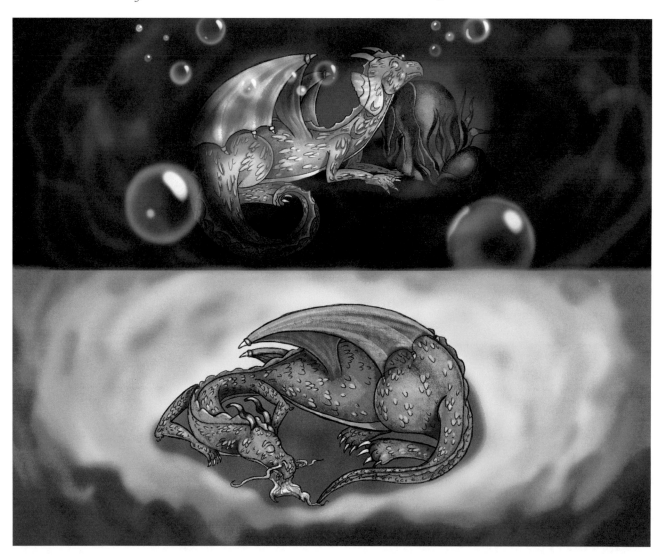

Chapter 4

THE DINOSAURS

The planet had changed immensely – unrecognizably so. Mother let her baby Dragons lay sleeping peacefully and the Fair Folk stayed retreated underground only coming up to tend to nature's cycle of life. Father Sky and Mother Earth felt the need to add a new group of creatures, so they created the dinosaurs that were much smaller than the Dragon children. These creatures ate either vegetation or flesh from another. They didn't have the same playful spirit as the Dragons either.

Along with the dinosaurs were the giant people who often tried to capture and eat the Fair Folk. However, they were never able to catch them because of the Fair Folk's ability to perform magick and disappear at the perfect time.

The brains of the dinosaurs and giants were extremely small, and they used only their instinct to survive. They did not have a conscience, nor did they possess discernment. They did not understand nature at all but lived for a million years until Father summoned another Ice Age and most all of these creatures became extinct following this event. On the other hand, the Fair Folk were able to read nature like a book, so they always survived any predicament.

This Ice Age lasted for a million or so years until the great thaw but as a reminder of this event the two poles stayed frozen and they were called the Artic and Antarctic. Occasionally, a frozen dinosaur will pop up in the ice. However, when the skeleton of any thirty-foot giants are found, it becomes a big secret... nobody speaks about them because they think they'll awaken other giants. To this day, the skeletons of these giants still are hidden from public view. And there's also a hush-hush shared amongst the Fair Folk when they found another colossal purplish egg. The Fair Folks buried it at the top of the highest mountain so it would be safe from all the elements and other beings.

Chapter 5

The Animal Kingdom

Father Sky and Mother Earth were busy creating new creatures and called them animals. Their first creation into the animal kingdom was the salmon of wisdom that swims in the clear sparkling deep blue waters; then the great eagle along with the hawk of dawn that flies in the pure fresh air above the clouds in the skies; then the majestic stag and his doe that runs swiftly through the forest; then the massive bear that lives in the fruitful north; and so on until all these animals balanced out in nature and worked in harmony with each other. These animals ate either vegetation or flesh just like the dinosaurs but on a much smaller scale. However, the salmon remained the most special of all creatures because after millions of years it always remembered from where it came from. Its offspring kept this valuable trait going in their bloodlines to this day. This is what distinguishes them as the wisest of all animal creatures.

Mother Earth called on Father Sky to discuss creating Human Beings who would be very different than all the other creatures. They would possess the gifts of instinct and free will. And just like the animals they would be able to reproduce other beings like themselves so there would be a male and female. Their size would be very small in comparison to the giants who walked with the dinosaurs.

She first placed them in the rainforest of what we know today as Africa and made them in the image of herself with dark skin, hair and eyes just like the richest fertile soil she ever produced. The mystical darkness of their brown eyes stood out against their white background just as the brightness of their brilliant white smile stood out against the background of their dark velvety skin tone. Stunningly beautiful and happy Human Beings they were.

They lived in harmony with the animal kingdom, as well as the Fair Folk. Everyone loved the Humans. They were curious and creative. They built tools and shelters out of mud, grass, sticks and stones. And they ate mostly grains and vegetation.

They were taught how to do prayers, ceremonies and rituals by the Fair Folk and learned some of their magickal ways. The Humans enjoyed singing, dancing and making music, as well as praying during their ceremonies and rituals.

The Fair Folk showed these Humans how to read the sun, moon and stars, listen to the wind, administer natural healing techniques and talk to the nature beings and spirits of the land. Humans caught on quickly and watched other animals' behavior and learned from them too. They communed with nature ever so well. They learned to plant and harvest food from the land leaving blessings of gratitude. And they made sure no one was left hungry. Humans also learnt when to move on, so they didn't wear out the land. Some traveled very far away from Africa and created diversified cultures that suited their adventurist and different lifestyles.

However, over hundreds of years, their images started to change. Some grew taller and some shorter. Some developed a different shaped face, nose, mouth and ears. Even their eyes changed shape displaying unusual colors of golden brown, grey, green or blue. And others hair turned to brown, red, yellow, white or gray. And some had olive, red, tan, brown, black, peach, pink, yellow or white skin. All these changes really didn't matter, everyone worked together in peace and harmony in their villages – taking pride in their contribution to life and each other. Most all tribes had a Chief, Priest or Priestess who was a very Wise Elder, as well as a Medicine Man or Medicine Women who looked after the tribe to make sure everyone stayed healthy.

They all lived by the Natural Laws of Nature and the Golden Rule.

Chapter 6

CHANGE IN THE HUMAN RACE

Then one day, a Human took the flesh of an animal and ate it. That changed the DNA of their offspring. They too became flesh eaters. Their peaceful ways started to shift, and they became more aggressive and selfish. The Fair Folk were very disappointed in the Human's behavior and didn't trust them anymore. The Fair Folk retreated into the hills and slipped between dimensions so most Humans could not see them anymore. This change created more change in the Human Race. Their instinct started to fade, and they were easily led astray. They started to depend on time from a clock to tell them where to go and what to do. They even created a calendar so they wouldn't forget what day it was.

At some point, a tall, brawny, red bearded man with dark brown eyes and handsome chiseled facial features appeared in a village. He announced that he was Byron, the King of the land and was coming to rule the people of the land. He demanded taxes from all the villagers. He hired guards who happened to be the strongest, but not the wisest men, in the village to protect him and collect these taxes from the peoples. He told these guards that they would be exempt from paying taxes for their loyalty to the King. He carried an air of superiority about him, so the villagers always paid their taxes without any question. They became slaves of King Byron. And the King never lifted a finger for a day's labor. Furthermore, this so-called King dreamed up unusual rules for the villagers to follow. King Byron had also sought out a woman who he called a Queen to be his wife. Of course, he chose the most beautiful woman in the village named Edwina. Edwina was very curvaceous, average in height with long flowing red hair. Her green eyes sparkled like emeralds and her perfectly round face had a light peachy complexion. She always wore a beautiful smile. They had several offspring and they called themselves the royal bloodline.

As the years went by, King Byron grew unhealthy by overeating and drinking way too much mead and ale. And Queen Edwina grew very bored with the King's obsession of counting all his riches many times a day. The Queen's eyes wandered for she longed for another's heart. He happened to be the village musician and storyteller, who called himself Ivan the Bard. Ivan the Bard was not only tall and slim but a stately gentleman with long blonde curly hair, blue eyes and sharp pointy facial features, not overly attractive in appearance but very, very charming. He knew how to easily charm another, including the King and Queen, with his silver tongue, quick wit, wonderful sense of humor, captivating stories and mesmerizing songs. Ivan the Bard loved to wear elaborate costumes when performing his arts. Even though the King enjoyed Ivan the Bards performances, he couldn't relax and fully enjoy the show due to his jealousy and insecurity. One day, he noticed how his Queen looked, smiled, winked and whispered in the ear of Ivan the Bard. King Byron went berserk, and he beheaded his Queen Edwina for what he assumed was infidelity.

The King was always fearfully waiting for the next contender to bequest the throne. And so, it was... there was another, King Erle, self-appointed in power that conquered the previous King Byron. This type of royal scam traveled to other villages and soon it became part of life. The village people followed the unusual rules and kept paying taxes to the gluttons and what one might even call freeloaders. They never once questioned their motives. So, as it goes, despondently the people gave up their free will along with their natural instincts.

Before long, the loving safety of the tribal connection that their wise Ancestors lived with was lost. The villagers grew apart from each other and learned to only take care of themselves. They became very submissive and only learnt what the folks 'in charge' wanted them to learn. It was nonsense. Sadly, they lost their ability to read the sun, moon and stars, as well as commune with nature. And without question, they raised animals for slaughter, farmed and mined gold and other minerals with the majority of the proceeds primarily going to those 'in charge'. *This submissive behavior has gone on for thousands of years now.* The Fair Folk often think; *"If only Humans would wake up and really see what's most important... like health, family, friends, community, neighbors and nature!"*

Chapter 7

Moving Ahead to the Present

Moving ahead to the present day... What the environment looks like today is quite a different story, with an overbuilt society, which has diminished much of the natural landscapes and replaced them with towering skyscrapers, big houses and housing projects. Several of the trees in the forests have been cut for no good reason other than for their lumber and with no set plans for their regrowth.

Trees are considered the lungs of the earth. They help filter the air and give us fresh oxygen. Without them we would be in really big trouble.

Some Humans have come to some of these sacred places like the rainforests and tried to push the Native Tribes of Indigenous Peoples out of their villages by claiming their natural resources for themselves. And sometimes they threaten their lives for things like oil, water, diamonds and gold.

Think about it ~ isn't it really silly that we have to pay for clean bottled water because most of water sources are polluted and by whom? Is it some of the same businesses that are now selling us the clean water? Why is oil more important than a clean water source? Where is all this oil coming from? ... Is it Coal as she lay sleeping? And why would diamonds and gold mean more than the life of another being? It looks like some Humans have forgotten how to live by 'The Golden Rule'. "Do unto others as you would have them do unto you."

The Indigenous Peoples, also called Natives, know that we do not own the land including the waters and air. And to them money doesn't mean anything – it's only a piece of paper with a promise of nothing really. Their Ancestors had been lied to and tricked into sharing or even giving up their lands. In return, they were given land that the old settlers could not handle living on, but the natives knew how to survive just about anywhere. However, their hearts were broken, and they felt betrayed. They were mostly saddened at seeing the loss of respect for both the lands and all the other nature beings of the lands.

What the Indigenous People have always followed is a life of living in ordinance with nature and they know it is the only way to survive on this planet in the long run. The Indigenous Peoples are native to the lands of their Ancestors and learned how to work in harmony with Mother Earth by using plant medicine and respectfully taking care of the land. They never forgot the teachings of their Ancestors and still teach their children to help one another, never ever take more than they need and pray with gratitude to the Great Spirit for everything that life offers them every day.

Actually, the Indigenous People are similar to the salmon of wisdom and know that their spirit will someday lie with their Ancestors in the sacred land in which they were born. They also know that all the conveniences society has created in life can be lost in a flash. And then what would society do? How would most people survive?

Over the last few decades, technology has filled our lives with a new way of instantly accessing information and communicating. In some ways it has made life easier for society and in other ways it has gradually distanced the intimate connections between people. It has helped several people on all levels via computers, machinery, robotics, motor vehicles, office work, etc. and taken jobs from others with the use of automation which minimizes human labor by using these same mechanical or electronic devices.

Countless devices have appeared to mesmerize and seduce mostly the younger population with its luring functions. In fact, several people strongly feel they can't live without their electronic devices...

Think about where you might fit into that scenario and if you weren't able to use any of your electronics for some strange reason... how would you live?

The balance and foresight of life has become 'out of control'. It might be a very good idea to say the Ho'oponopono Prayer for all the Ancestors who ever walked before us and those that need love and forgiveness. It goes like this – *"I'm sorry; Please forgive me; Thank you; I love you!"* It is a simple but extremely powerful prayer and can be said over and over and over again. With repentance, forgiveness, gratitude and love; we can heal our Ancestors' deep wounds and it can heal ours too. It also helps one to say the Ho'oponopono Prayer for someone who has wronged them and they have been feeling very bitter about it. Bitterness is an awful ugly feeling to hold onto. It also steals smiles from people's faces and turns them into a grumpy curmudgeon. And bitterness, if held onto for a long period of time, can sadly wither the heart.

Life is never constant. Everything we do today will effect tomorrow, as well as years to come. If something is corrupt, we have a few choices – join in, walk away and hide from it or outright ask them why they are doing it. If we allow things we do not like to happen without saying anything then we have taken part in it as a witness. Sometimes saying something at the moment is not an option. Always listen to your 'gut' feelings so if you cannot say anything at the time because it's not safe, then you need to find someone you can trust to tell like a Parent, Grandparent, Aunt, Uncle, Neighbor, Teacher, Social Worker, Police, Rabbi, Minister, Preacher, Priest or anyone who's considered trustworthy. And how can we change all the bad news to good news? Turn it off or maybe just choose to listen or watch only uplifting information instead of a depressing, fearful and horrible newsflash. Feed your mind and soul with good and inspirational info!

Nature beings have always chosen to work with the W.I.T.C.H. by helping them 'Work In The Community Healing' using nature's plentiful gifts. Each nature being has its own recipe for healing... so there are many ways to heal using different elements of nature. And with the right combination anything can be healed. However only the ones connected to the heart of nature can ever be true healers! The Indigenous Peoples, Witches, Druids, Shamans, Naturopaths, Herbalists, Eco-therapists, Gardeners and Children are the Fair Folk and Nature Beings favorite Humans. If more Humans connected their heart to nature and became healers, then there would be more love and less fighting over trivial things.

The world is openly waiting for positive change, and it is up to us to be that positive change. Ask yourself this profound question; "How can I serve the betterment of this planet?" What comes to mind? We the people can unite together and become stronger with constructive ways to help each other and the planet.

Many people are already starting this movement by biodynamic farming, growing organic community gardens, planting trees, creating solutions for recycling waste, forming prayer groups, paying it forward with unexpected good deeds, helping others in need by giving them food, clothing, first aid and shelter, volunteering at their favorite charity events and just being kind, friendly and cheerful.

Being good in action and doing good in will... where there's a will there's a way... *It is doable!* There is hope however, at the close of this tale there's a warning...

Warning: It is whispered between the realms that the Dragon Sisters must not be awakened because this planet has changed so much over these billions of years. If Coal, with her hot temper, woke first, this planet just might be burnt to a crisp due to the fact that Mother Earth would be unrecognizable to her and she might react in a fierce way.

Most of society wouldn't stand a chance of survival because there would be no room on the planet for either of the Dragons to roam. However, perhaps wakening a Dragon or two would move things along and help create a change for the betterment of Mother Earth... Befriending a Dragon might be extremely empowering.

Wouldn't it be awesome to work alongside a Dragon finding solutions to clean up all Mother Earth's natural resources by making miracles happen!

So then, on second thought, maybe the Dragon Sisters should be awakened. *What do you think we should do? Wake the Dragon Sisters or let them sleep...*

GLOSSARY:

All mythical beings (a.k.a. fair folk, nature spirits or elementals) once lived in total harmony with each other and nature. They all had special gifts as well as super human power and strength. Many of them worked alongside each other taking care of nature with special jobs they loved doing. They never complained ever. Over the years many of them have mastered the magick of shape-shifting, bending time and physical laws, and creating rapid manifestations and miracles. It also became easy for them to slip between realms, dimensions, portals, veils, vortexes, ley lines and time. Actually time didn't mean much to any of them as they were more interested in seasons and changes in the weather patterns. In fact, several of them influenced those changes and still do. Humans once corresponded with these beings, but because of the way many of the humans showed disrespect for nature the elemental beings just stopped associating with them. Sadly, some of the elemental beings also picked up negative traits that humans portrayed like greed, anger, grumpiness and even fighting with each other usually over territory. Today, these magickal beings are usually seen either if a human is kind especially to nature or harming nature in any way. However, they are not a force to be reckoned with especially if one is disrespectful to Mother Nature.

BROWNIES – a.k.a Kobolds. They are dwarf size beings that have the appearance of wrinkled skin, pointed facial features, large ears and nose, brown shaggy sometimes curly hair and wore brown or drab green tattered clothes. They spend most of their time outside during all kinds of weather and many reside in either the hollow of an older tree or near waterways like streams or waterfalls. Brownies are usually introverts, preferring alone time however they love to work at night caretaking to the creatures of the forest.

DRAGONS – uncommon name usually used in ancient writing was Draegon. Although Dragons occur in many legends around the world, different cultures have varying stories about monsters that have been grouped together under the dragon label. Dragons have been acknowledged for thousands of years in many cultures like Ancient Samaria, Asia, Africa, Egypt, Scandinavia, Greenland, Greece, the Celtic Lands, Great Britain and even Mexico. The appearance of Dragons varies but mostly resemble gigantic lizards, crocodiles, dinosaurs, snakes and even sea creatures and their heads were often described with similarities to that of lions or goats. Because of their strong relationship to serpentine or reptilian it is said that their offspring's hatch from eggs. Some have leathery bat-like wings, beards, long cloven tongue, large red or gold eyes, either no legs, two legs or four legs, webbed feet, three, four or five claws, fangs, horns, hoods, multi-heads, fins, scales, spiny protrusions or a combination of these features. They are known to breathe and spit different things, like fire, poison or ice vapor. Their massive bodies are often described with some similarities yet fashioned in many colors. And they're always portrayed as magickal, fierce, loyal, protective and territorial. Dragons love to make their homes in castles, forest groves, mountains, deserts, caves, springs or certain parts of the sea. Dragons are often held to have major, spiritual significance in various religions and cultures around the world. In many East Asian cultures, dragons are revered as representative of the primal forces of nature. With a strong connection to nature and the elements, Dragons for the most part, are linked to cleansing nature with natural disasters including tsunamis, hurricanes, earthquakes and volcanoes, as well as bad weather patterns like thunder and electrical storms. They're known to be intuitive and have above-average intelligence. Dragons primarily symbolized courage, strength, endurance, power, protection, wisdom and longevity. One of the ancient Chinese secrets was that to be living in accord with nature was a safe way to befriend a Dragon!

DRYADS – a.k.a. Tree Nymphs. The Tree Nymphs partook of the distinguishing characteristics of the particular tree to whose life they're committed and are known collectively by the name of the Dryads. Basically, they're spirits who dwell in trees with a great love for oaks in particular. They hold magick and wisdom, so they're often contacted by Druids and Shamans for inspiration.

ELVES – Elves eventually moved to Middle Earth which lies deep within the forest and exists simultaneously on many planes. Elves like to live in groups, you will rarely find a solitary elf, they are very social and when the opportunity arises, they will even be friendly towards mortals. They also communicate with each other telepathically. Elves are generally tall, slender, graceful and extremely strong, as well as ambidextrous with four fingers on each hand and four toes on each foot, pointed ears and sharp features. All Elves are part of the family and always greet one another with great big hugs. Almost all elves are bisexual and are not attracted primarily by physical appearance. It is believed that this is because elven men and women look more or less the same, and they are all beautiful. Neither sex has any body hair, and no difference in voice pitch. There are many varieties of elves such as Woodland Elves, Fire Elves, Gray Elves, Green Elves, Blue Elves, Gold Elves, Silver Elves, Blessed Elves, Wind Elves, River Elves, Sea Elves, Highland Elves, Lowland Elves, Hill Elves, Forest Elves, Mountain Elves and Meadow Elves. Their coloration as a whole varies wildly because their coloration often matches their surroundings. So really depending on where Elves are from also depends on what color skin and hair they have. Their hair color usually ranged from silver, white, blonde, brown, black and auburn. Their eyes are wide and almond-shaped, and filled with large, vibrantly colored pupils that are mostly grey or hazel green and sometimes brown or blue. Some even developed different physical characteristics to adapt to the immediate needs of their environments like gills for the Sea Elves. All Elves are nature lovers, blending into the environment naturally becoming at one with the Earth. And they are resistant to extremes of nature, illness and disease. Elves do not age and they don't sleep however they meditate in trance for a few moments and then enter the world of dreams fully awake. The entirety of the elven life is one of fun, love, laughter, creativity and childlike playfulness. Elves also have an innate gift for craftsmanship and artistry, as well as an appreciation for the written word and magick. Within elven society, wizards are held in extremely high regard as masters of an art both powerful and aesthetically valued. Their naturally keen minds and senses, combined with their inborn patience, make them particularly suited to wizardry. Elves strongly live their lives with these virtues; a love of freedom, a strong sense of personal responsibility by keeping their promises, and do not form particular attachments easily. However, their magickal possessions are the big exception. They also love music, celebrations, dancing, gifts and flowers in the garden. Plants love to harmonize with Elves as they sing the song of the universe. Elves have a deep love of trees because they are directly related to them. They tell the story of their ancestors who originating from Ah and Kin, the first great trees who died and became the first Elves. Ah and Kin stood atop the world and fruited the Sun, Moon, Seas, Stars and various plants, animals and other nature beings including the Elves. This was the way all things grew and ripened, fell off the branches and onto the ground of being. Once there, they crawled or moved to different parts of the world, where they were born from the seed, pod, egg or womb of their parents. Ah and Kin were what humans might call 'gods' and the Elves call 'The Elders', 'The Ancient Ones', 'The Celestial Masters', 'The Old Ones', or countless other names of endearment. Both Elves and Fairies have supernatural powers, allowing them to move through space and change their shape into any form they choose and while in the fairy realm, Elves and Fairies are immortal. Due to their long lifespans, Elves can expect to remain active in the same location for centuries. Elves seek to live in balance with the wild and their keen sense helps them to maintain sustainable lifestyles. They have a keen understanding of working with nature, rather than attempting to bend it to their will. These nature spirits are all around, so beware, they repay kindheartedness with kindheartedness and misbehavior with misbehavior. So, where Elves and Fairies are concerned one gets what they give tenfold. Elves are very protective towards nature and the Earth, and they want humans to take more care of the Earth as well as become more in touch with nature. The Fairy and Elf realm is carefully hidden; however, dusk is the time to see Elves. They love the Moon and celebrate the Moon when it rises. Children are more likely than adults to catch sight of these magnificent nature spirits.

FAIRIES – a.k.a. Sidhe, Fae, Fay, Faery, Faerie, Wee Folk, Fair Folk, Good Folk, People of Peace, The Cousins. Over the years, Fairies have gone by many descriptions and have many regional characteristics, but in Britain and Ireland they are known mostly as Faeries, the Sidhe, the Gentry, the Shining Ones, and in later folklore, the dismissive title of 'the Little People', in an attempt to play down their power and importance to critical Catholic clergy. Faeries are beings of spirit that have no solid bodily substance per say and have the capability to change form (shape-shift) at will for a variety of reasons. And have always been able to display infinite power and supernatural abilities such as the capability to fly, glow in the dark, cast spells and conjure up gold as well as being able to influence or foresee the future. Fairies love to show up in the appearance of tiny, cute, colorful, often winged beings (kinda like a dragonfly or a pixie) in appearance with petite but sharp features. Their swift movement makes them look like flashes of colors bouncing from flower to flower or place to place. Faeries are intimately connected to the soul of Mother Earth, and they draw in and direct energy straight from Source/ God/Goddess, as it manifests from Mother Earth's spiritual heart. They form extremely strong bonds with nature. Fairies watch over and protect the natural world – woodlands, trees, rivers, plants and animals. They live in the invisible realms of every forest, flower, mountainside, rock and tree (especially hollow trees). Fairies are the ones who make the flowers blossom. Fairies are nature's artists, and they adore all that they consider beautiful which is shown by their passion with art, song, poetry, music, celebrations, and dance. They love gifts and flowers in the garden but never cut flowers as that would be an insult to them. The Fairies, Elves and other magickal beings hold nightly parties filled with dancing, singing, storytelling, and laughter. Some have mentioned that they've been known to dance on the hillsides every night for eternity. They have a perky playful liveliness about them, and they're drawn to positive loving energies. They know the spiritual value of playfulness and joy! It is said that Fairy energy signatures vibrate at a very different, yet compatible rate to our own. And their proximity to us causes our energy fields to become altered, opening up whole new channels of awareness for us to experience by encouraging an awareness of something far more expansive and profound. Fairies favor the essence of honey, cake, cream, milk, nectar, sweet butter, chocolate or candy. Offerings of shinny things and silver mercury head dimes as well as song, music and dance are well loved by Faeries. They also adore silliness so singing 'nonsense' songs and drawing your inspiration ('awen' in the Welsh and 'imbas' in Irish) from the natural world and trying to give voice to the spirits of the surrounding land. Be open to their magick and remember to be very respectful in all your dealings with Fairies, and you shall in time, be gifted with allies and Faerie friends that may accompany you and your family for generations. Most importantly, offerings should always be biodegradable and not ruin the environment you are attempting to honor as sacred. Clearing an area of rubbish or pollution is an excellent offering and is always appreciated by all surrounding nature spirits as well as the Faeries. And avoid any iron work which disrupts the natural flow of their energy, but bronze, copper and silver have the opposite effect by healing the energy flow, and attracting Faeries and nature spirits of all kinds.

FIRE SPIRITS – a.k.a. Salamanders. They have the appearance of a lizard or dragon usually a glowing orange in color and live in the heart of a fire. Fire Spirits are fierce and relentless. They demand attention and respect for their powers, or they'll engulf their surroundings with their wrath. They are connected to the Djinn or Genies that can sometimes appear from the smoke and are seen as massive blue creatures. When one looks really deep into the heart of a fire, they'll see a blue flame burning brightly… is that the Djinn dancing?

GNOMES – nature spirits who serve at the earthly physical level. Gnomes are considered earth dwellers or earth elementals that love the direction of North. Gnomes tend the earth through the cycles of the four seasons and see to it that all living things in nature are supplied with their daily needs. It is said that Gnomes might have originated in Scandinavia and then traveled to Germany before settling in other countries throughout. Over the years, Gnomes have evolved and become a very widespread species and also consist of a number of different types. Because they're dwarf in size about a foot or two tall and pigeon toed, they're able to move through solid earth easily as if it was air. The Gnomes favorite piece of attire is their red peaked felted cap and they like to wear colorful felted clothing but at one time their clothing was mostly neutral colors. A male gnome will generally wear a small tool-belt around his waist, just in case something needs fixing and often smoke a pipe. The female Gnomes always keeps her hair braided but wears a scarf over her head under

her cap. They wear a blouse and skirt with an apron along with felted shoes. Most are nocturnal. Because they're completely incapable of worrying, gnomes never grow bald or have heart attacks, and can live as long as 400 years. As a rule, gnomes are more than 7 times stronger than humans, and can run much faster (about 35 miles an hour). They even have better sight than a hawk. Although Gnomes are considered serious, they have elevated practical jokes to an art form. The Gnomes are the most serious and hardworking of all the fair folk. Male Gnomes are the guardians of the animal and mineral kingdom. Mining precious gems and metals are their favorite thing to do so they usually wear a tool belt, carry a shovel or push a wheelbarrow. They're gentle by nature and are considered a vegetarian with their favorite foods being mushrooms, tubers, nuts, peas, beans, vegetables, fruit especially berries and honey mead. Gnomes tend to live in hilly meadows and rocky woodlands. They re-cycle and process the waste by-products of nature and purge the earth of poisons and pollutants that are dangerous to life on earth. Their enemies are any beings who would try to destroy them, their friends, and their homes or disrespect anything in Mother Nature. Otherwise, for the most part, they're usually peaceful beings. It has been said that if you befriend a Gnome they will bring you abundance and good fortune.

LIMONIADES – a.k.a. Meadow Nymphs. They are usually represented frolicking and dancing hand in hand in a circle. They are cute and tiny in size. Their deep love for the Earth is expressed with their adoration of plants and flowers, and they are extremely dedicated to the beautification of the Earth on all levels.

LEPRECHAUNS – are part of the Tuatha De Danann (type of people in Irish Folklore), always male, and best described as a short, wizened, red bearded old man who usually dresses in a green suit with a large gold buckle on its belt, and a green top hat in which a golden four-leaf clover (a symbol of good luck), is tucked into a gold buckled black band. However, it is said that their first ancestors were clad in red and wore a tri-cornered hat. They're seen sporting spiffy black buckled shoes, and often wearing a leather apron as well as smoking a pipe. They like to make their homes in abandoned burrows, hollow trees, caves with openings that are hidden by bushes and trees. Leprechauns like to inhabit places that do not draw attention to them because they're primarily solitary creatures who spend their time as cobblers of the fairy world, making and mending shoes. It's been said that Leprechauns dance the Irish jig so much they wear out their shoes. Leprechauns have a distinctive sound associated with them, recognized by the tap-tap-tapping of a tiny cobbler hammer, driving nails into a shoe, which announces they are near. They can be mischievous but harmless little creatures and store their gold coins in a pot of gold that is hidden at the end of a rainbow. Some legends say leprechaun carry one gold coin for every year they have been alive. Other fables say if a human catches a leprechaun that leprechaun must grant that human three wishes in exchange for his freedom. However, they are tricky and quick as a wink and always outsmart their captures. It has been noted that they reward kindness with gifts of gold – so be kind!

MER-PEOPLE – are from the Undine family. The upper half of their bodies is human in form and the lower half with an iridescent fish-like scaled tail. They're mostly seen as Mermaids with an appearance of an attractive female with long flowing hair from the waist up and an iridescent scaled fish tail from the waist down. They adorn themselves with seashells, seaweed and other beautiful objects from the sea.

NIXIES – are spirits who dwell in quiet rivers and lakes. Their true loves are water and song. Their beautiful angelic voices are often accompanied by musical instruments. Their mesmerizing song can easily draw listeners to the banks of their watery homes. Nixies are female and Nix are male in form. These water spirits are avid shapeshifters and can take on any appearance they want, such as a similarity to humans, mer-people, snakes, fish, horses or even a sunken treasure. In human form, they usually have an elegant appearance and often dress in stylish garments. Although their features might hint at their wilder natures, their ears and eyes are sharper than usual, and their hair and skin might be tinted with green or blue. In more extreme cases, they can have gills, bulbous eyes, and webbed hands and feet. When they're in an animal form, Nixies replace the charms of their music with dazzling physical beauty. As a pure white horse, they can hypnotize onlookers by prancing around, flaunting their mane and tail. Even though they can come onto land, these creatures can't bear separation from water for a great length of time.

NYMPHS – are the presiding deities of the woods, grottoes, streams, meadows, etc. These divinities appear as beautiful maidens of fairy-like form, robed in more or less shadowy garments. Nymphs are associated with producing sweet sounding music. They're held in the greatest veneration, though, being minor divinities, they have no temples dedicated to them, but are worshipped in caves or grottoes, with libations of milk, honey, oil, etc.

PIXIES – are wee, merry, magical creatures. They are beloved for their childlike appearance and effervescent spirit; however, they are known to be pranksters and occasionally tricksters. One might compare their sense of humor to that of a Gnome. These little people have a special talent for casting charms. Plants grow more quickly, flowers blossom more brightly, and wild animals are tame when they are nurtured by Pixies. Their skin may be flesh-colored, blue, or green. Their eyes and ears are slightly pointed, and they have exquisite wings that resemble a butterfly. Unless they dress in a leaf or flower from the plant kingdom, they go around naked. Pixies are meadow and woodland creatures where some live in ancient underground locations like barrows (mounds of earth covering a burial ground), which usually have some connection to their ancestors. Other locations might be stone rings, hollowed trees or tree stumps.

SELKIES – are usually smaller seals that live in the sea and can shapeshift by removing their coats to become an attractive human when they desire to walk on land.

SYLPHS – are generally small, beautiful, sprightly, ageless beings who energetically move with aerial grace. They are known to be cheery, eccentric, etheric shapeshifters who enjoy dancing in the wind. Their creative passions are cloud forming and designing snowflakes as well as decorating the earth with beautifully falling leaves. Their elements are air, gases, and ether and they love to surf through life on the currents of wind.

TROLLS – can be either a giant or a dwarf in size and prefer to be scantily clad. Typically, they're cave-dwelling beings and sometimes live underground in a hillside or under bridges. Trolls communicate by a variety of different grunting sounds. Although they are not considered very intelligent, Trolls frequently possess great treasures of gold, silver and gemstones in their caves or underground residences. Their appearance has been described to be somewhat homely in looks with unruly long greasy hair, greenish skin, and yellowish teeth with two tusks on the bottom row, a very large mouth, nose and ears, small beady eyes, a big belly, four-fingered hands with long yellowish finger nails and enormous feet with only three toes per foot. They are very muscular and heavy-set often with a crooked back or sometimes with several heads. Female Trolls have a much smaller physique than males and the older females have long saggy breasts. The older Troll males will often have long beards and a very hairy body especially their back, forearms and legs. Both sexes of the older Trolls will also often develop many warts, which are considered to be a sign of beauty among Trolls, and they grow even more obese and wrinkled with age. They also possess the ability to transform themselves into logs or tree stubs on a whim.

UNDINES – The Undine group contains many species also known as Mermaids – upper half female and lower half fish with long flowing hair; Naiades – a type of female spirit, or nymph, who preside over fountains, wells, springs, streams, brooks, lakes and other bodies of fresh water; Selkies - often seen as seals that can change into an incredibly handsome and beautiful human form; Water Nymphs a.k.a. Water Sprites – elemental guardian of water. As a whole, their stunning appearance closely resembles a female human in size and form (excluding the Water Nymphs who resemble Fairies). They all have long flowing hair and are smaller in frame. They're known to be sensitive and most are friendly. They make their homes in anything containing water such as waterfalls, rivers, marshes and fens, mountain lakes, and ocean waves. They can be found in coral caves under the sea and under lily pads, as well as mosses beneath the waterfall.

WATER SPRITES – a.k.a. Water Nymph or Water Fairy. They are a rather small elemental spirit associated with water and are said to be able to breathe water or air and also possess the ability to fly. Water Sprites are known as the elemental guardians of water. They look after the rivers and the animals that live within it. Water Sprites are mostly harmless unless threatened. They are very playful, and it is said that one can feel their excitable energy especially near shallow fast flowing water or in the surf. Water Sprites energetically purify the water and have been known to infuse a healing frequency into certain waters such as sacred wells. They are very susceptible to human mismanagement of their homes. When rivers get dirty the energy of the land and everything around it is lowered so this energy depletion means that disease and illness sets in. Sprites play a vital role in the energy systems of all the ecosystems in the world.

DEFINITION OF HEALERS:

BARDS – are one of three types or orders of Druids. Bards are the brilliant entertainers who mastered the spoken word with poetry, songs, music and stories that they shared orally with the tribe.

DRUIDS – early history remains a mystery, as our knowledge is based on limited records primarily due to their oral tradition. However, Druids were first made reference too many thousands of years ago for their organized intellectual lifestyle as well as being a highly respected culture amongst society. Quick witted and scholarly, the Druids were considered the wisest and most learned people of their time. Being a Druid was considered a tribal function with equal status to both males and females. Amongst the tribe were gifted poets, musicians, astronomers, magicians, judges, doctors, herbalists, priests, priestesses, alchemists, teachers and astrologers. It took most Druids 20 or more years to learn their lore by heart as druids preferred oral teaching to writing. And they were the ones who acted as advisors to local political leaders. The Druids had the privileges of not paying taxes or serving in battle. They even had the ability to come between two opposing armies and prevent warfare. These particular Celts had developed a highly sophisticated polytheistic spiritual/religious system and magickal practice with three types or orders of Druids: the Bards, brilliant entertainers who mastered the spoken word with poetry, songs, music and stories that they shared orally with the tribe, the Ovates, who were the healers, seers, astrologers, astronomers, mathematicians, alchemists, wizards and magicians, and the Druids, who were the scholars, philosophers, judges and teachers. It is said that the Druids' principal doctrine was that the soul was immortal and passed at death from one person into another. All aspects of Druidism were well structured and ordered; from the hierarchy of the Druid class (Arch-Druid), to their pattern of life that followed nature's cycles to survive in a sacred and prosperous way. The practice of Druidry today holds true, as each clan member's first and foremost duty is taken as a vow of being a "steward of the earth". The Druids observe lunar, solar and seasonal cycles and worship according to these on 8 major holy days; *Samhain – 10/31 New Years, Yule – Winter Solstice, Imbolc – 2/2 Feast Of Lights, Ostara – Spring Equinox, Beltaine – 5/1 Spring Fertility Festival, Litha – Summer Solstice, Lughnasa – 8/2 First Harvest, Mabon – Autumn Equinox.* They hold ceremonies in hallowed places like secluded groves of trees, caves, stone circles or remote valleys. The Druids have a deep connection to trees especially the mighty oak. Pagan, Wiccan and Druid studies are all intertwined in the web of nature, healing, alchemy and spiritual practices. To this day, Druidry is considered a living spirituality that holds all of Nature sacred, and offers a path of creativity and freedom, with deep roots in an ancient Celtic-Druidic Shamanic tradition.

ECO-THERAPISTS – a.k.a. "green therapy" or "earth-centered therapy." According to Howard Clinebell, who wrote a 1996 book on this topic of "Eco-therapy" which he refers to the healthy interaction with the earth. Eco-therapy corresponds with the belief that people are part of the web of life and that our psyches are not secluded or separate from our environment. Eco-therapy is based on the idea that people are connected to and impacted by the natural environment. Connection with the Earth and its natural systems are the heart of eco-therapy. Most Eco-therapists consider that the Earth has a healing capacity which operates through complex systems of integrated balance, and that if a person can harmonize with these systems, they may experience improved mental health. Both personal and planetary well-being is not separate from each other. The beneficial effects of nature result not only from what people see but from what they experience through other senses as well. Humans crave the comfort of nature in the same way that a child needs a mother. Relationships of healing with nature, place, creatures, and Earth require us to acknowledge our participation in industrial, governmental, or organizational actions that harm the environment and to seek alternative actions whenever possible. However, within the last century many of us have been confined to man-made environments. Beginning with the Industrial Revolution, people have been steadily removed from the natural world, our lives regulated not by the lunar, solar and seasonal cycles but instead by the time clock. As technology advances, with the rise of the Internet and social media, it's gotten worse, consuming our lives, programing society away from nature. People are worrying themselves sick over the impending threat of environmental disaster. According to behaviorists, this phenomenon has been coined "eco-anxiety," and those who have it experience real symptoms, such as panic attacks, sleeplessness, loss of appetite and depression. Connecting more with nature can help improve depression, anxiety, stress, lower blood pressure, improve self-esteem, decrease recovery time and help with impulse control. What kind of relationship you have with the natural world? Are you doing anything to help the environment? Are you stuck in an office or school all day? Do you get outside much? Eco-therapists believe that spending time outdoors is important for our health and suggest that additional benefit can be gained by augmenting these approaches with activities such as gardening, walking or other outdoor exercise, or spending time with animals. Another form of eco-therapy occurs when we bring nature indoors, in the form of indoor gardens, potted plants, or natural lighting.

HERBALISTS – a.k.a. herbal practitioners and licensed herbalists are specially trained in the field of herbal medicine. Plants have been the basis for medical treatments through much of human history. Herbalism, also called herbal medicine, botanical medicine, or phytomedicine, has been used for thousands of years. An herbalist uses plants, seeds, berries, roots, leaves, bark, and flowers of plants called herbs or botanicals for medicinal purposes to improve health, promote healing, and prevent and treat illness. When used as directed by a licensed herbalist, most herbal supplements are safe and do not cause adverse side effects. Herbalists take a holistic approach to medicine, which means that they focus on comprehensive health care that addresses the physical, mental, emotional, social, spiritual, as well as the economic needs of the patient. The scope of herbal medicine is sometimes extended to include fungal and bee products, as well as minerals or shells.

INDIGENOUS PEOPLES

– a.k.a. First Peoples/ Nations, Aboriginal Peoples, Native Peoples, Tribes, or Autochthonous Peoples, are ethnic groups who are the 'original inhabitants' (several thousand years) of a given region, in contrast to other groups that have settled, occupied or colonized the area more recently (few hundred years). These original inhabitants call themselves by many names in their 4,000 plus unique languages and constitute approximately 5% of the world's population. Indigenous peoples live in all regions of the world and own, occupy or use some 22% of global land area. Numbering at least 370-500 million of the population, Indigenous Peoples represent the better part of the world's cultural diversity and have created and speak the major share of the world's almost 7000 languages. Within their occupational and geographical positions, they're seen by each other as hunter-gatherers, nomads, peasants, hill people, warriors, etc. Indigenous Peoples are the holders of unique languages, knowledge systems and beliefs and possess invaluable awareness of practices for the sustainable management of natural resources. They are inheritors, stewards and practitioners of unique cultures using ancient traditions by primarily practicing sacred ways of relating to the spirits of the land, ancestors, healing, ceremony, community and environment along with its inhabitants – plant, animal and mineral kingdom. The land of their ancestors has a fundamental importance for their collective physical and cultural survival as peoples and their future generations. Indigenous Peoples hold their own diverse concepts of development, based on their traditional values, visions, needs and priorities. For the most part, Indigenous Peoples have retained unique political, social and economic characteristics, as well as cultural distinctiveness from each other including a difference in dress, religion (ceremony) and language that are distinct from other tribes. Despite their cultural differences, Indigenous Peoples from around the world share common problems related to the protection of their rights as distinct peoples of the land – their land. It is estimated that Indigenous territories contain 80 percent of the earth's biodiversity primarily due to the Indigenous people's stewardship and sacred relationship with the environment. Yet these regions face an unprecedented and rapid loss of biodiversity and climate change effects resulting from the fossil fuel-based industrialized global economy and natural resource extraction (mining, oil exploration, logging, and agro-industrial projects). Indigenous peoples have sought recognition of their identities, way of life and their right to traditional lands, territories and natural resources for years. However, throughout history their rights have been usually violated. Indigenous Peoples resist this invasion with tremendous courage and skill, but their protests are too often ignored by governments and corporations. The international community now recognizes that special measures are required to protect their rights and maintain their distinct cultures and way of life by engaging in modern technologies, education and joining forces with other Indigenous communities. For Indigenous Peoples, conservation of biodiversity is an integral part of their lives and is viewed as spiritual and functional foundations for their identities and cultures. Studies have shown that when the World Wildlife Fund listed the top 200 areas with the highest and most threatened biodiversity; they found that 95 percent are on

Indigenous territories. Often culturally, linguistically and geographically separate Indigenous Peoples from mainstream cultures. They also lack the financial resources, education and access to decision-making platforms to demand a voice at the table and ensure that their best interests are represented. Many Indigenous Peoples continue to be confronted with marginalization, extreme poverty and other human rights violations. Through partnerships with Indigenous Peoples, UNESCO, the United Nations Educational, Scientific and Cultural Organization, is a specialized agency of the United Nations system. UNESCO's mission is to contribute to the building of peace, the eradication of poverty, sustainable development and intercultural dialogue through education, the sciences, culture, communication and information. Another organization called "Cultural Survival" empowers and supports Indigenous Peoples to advocate for their rights — human rights, the right to participate and have a voice, the right to practice their cultures and speak their languages, the right to access the same opportunities as others, and the right to control and sustainably manage their assets and resources — so that they may determine for themselves the future they will lead, as well as the future they will leave for many generations to come.

NATUROPATHS – use a distinct system of primary health care that above all emphasizes prevention and also supports the self-healing process through the use of natural therapies. While its roots date back to 1890, naturopathic medicine has rapidly increased in public interest as a result to assist with the overwhelming amount of health care problems by using prevention for wellness. Naturopaths a.k.a. Naturopathic physicians or Naturopathic doctors (NDs) are primary care physicians who combine a variety of centuries-old knowledge. Some of the therapeutic modalities used in naturopathic medicine include clinical and laboratory diagnostic testing, nutritional medicine (diet), botanical medicine, herbalism, homeopathy, hydrotherapy, naturopathic physical manipulative therapy, public health measures, hygiene, psychology and spiritual counseling, minor surgery, exercise, acupuncture, massage, prescription medication, intravenous and injection therapy, and naturopathic obstetrics (natural childbirth), as well as integrating conventional, scientific and practical methodology with the ancient laws of nature. NDs identify and remove obstacles or the underlying causes of illness, rather than merely suppress symptoms to recovery. They most often utilize methods and medicinal substances which minimize the risk of harmful side effects, with the least force necessary to diagnose and treat their patients. NDs help facilitate the innate healing ability in patients through education as well as encouraging self-responsibility for their own health. NDs treat each individual as a 'whole' person by taking into account physical, mental, emotional, genetic, environmental and social factors. NDs emphasize the prevention of disease by assessing risk factors, heredity and susceptibility to disease, and by making appropriate interventions in partnership with their patients to prevent illness. Today, many NDs call themselves Functional Medical Doctors.

SHAMANS – are priests or priestesses who act as intermediary between the natural and supernatural worlds. They use magic for the purpose of curing the sick, divining the unseen and controlling spiritual forces. They live by a sacred way of life with reverence to their ancestors and an exceptionally strong connection with nature and all of creation. Shamanism can be best described as the ancient spiritual practices of indigenous cultures worldwide and can also be viewed as the universal spiritual wisdom inherent to all indigenous tribes. As all ancient spiritual practices are rooted in nature, Shamanism is the method by which we as human beings can strengthen that natural connection as a medium between the visible and spirit worlds. Shamans are considered a combination of a Holy man and a Medicine man/ woman.

WITCHES – 'Witch' the word in itself means 'wise woman'. Their wisdom shed light on the importance of loving one another "with harm to none". Throughout history and to this day, Witches practice their craft from deep within the heart and by communing with nature. Historically, Witches were known as the mediators between the human beings and the mysterious superpowers such as spirits, angels, Gods and Goddesses. When a Witch succeeded in resolving the apparently mysterious problem of someone, the performance was termed as magick. As a rule, Witches prayed to the higher powers or the spirits for help and guidance in resolving the problem by performing certain rituals and the whole process was called Witchcraft. In the ancient times, Witchcraft was known as 'craft of the wise' as the wise persons were those who followed the path of nature and were in tune with its forces, had the knowledge of herbs and medicines, gave wise counsel and were held in high esteem as Shamanic healers and leaders in the village and community. Many were known as a Witch Doctor. They understood that nature was superior to human beings and that human beings were simply one of the many parts of nature, both seen and unseen that combine to form one whole. Witchcraft, an earth-based religion, was practiced in almost all the societies and cultures across the world according to local beliefs and traditions. The acronym of W.I.T.C.H. means 'Work In The Community Healing'. It's unfortunate, that eventually Witches became condemned and the once respected name 'Witch' became tarnished with accusations of evil satanic practices by a male dominated society during the rise of Christianity. The world in the middle ages was rigidly religious peppered with wars, distrust and the belief that everything good or bad came from God. This was at a time when most of society was led to believe that God ruled man, and nature was there for us to exploit for profit. Sadly, their fears lead them to Witch-hunting and destroying mainly women who showed any signs of healing or being intuitive. Their belief that a Witch was a person who practices sorcery and sorcery can include a variety of aspects such as intuition, healing, divination, magic, alchemy, necromancy, spells, herbs, meditation, etc. 'Wise women' were drawn to the art of healing by their love of flowers and nature. They had an affinity with the natural and supernatural world that many people back then didn't even know existed. The 'wise woman' would have an abundance of flowers, herbs, plants and fruit in her garden. She used her knowledge of her garden's flora to make possets, which were hot drinks made from milk that was curdled, Ale, herbs and spices, fruit and honey. And she would add whatever herb or plant remedy that she believed would be helpful to heal any villagers who were sick. Many people who lived near the 'wise woman' would always go to her to be healed. And rosemary was the favorite of all 'wise women'. The reason was because they were not so hygienic back then and a sprig of rosemary, or a rosemary posy, also known as a nosegay, for obvious reasons, was a perfect remedy against the awful smells of the day. But rosemary really was a cure all plant as it stimulates appetite, helps to produce gastric juices and alleviates flatulence, alleviates headaches, aids pain from rheumatism, increases circulation, stimulate the hair follicles to help growth, and is used as an astringent. Ginger, cloves and cinnamon were the main ingredients to ward of colds and flu.

Other flowers and plants that were prized in the garden would be violets, honeysuckle, primroses, cowslips and wallflowers. The 'wise woman' would use these to make medicines, teas, conserves and jellies. Performing alchemy, the 'wise woman' would spend hours each day using pestle and mortar crushing and bruising the flowers or herbs, mixing and boiling the potions and hanging out the herbs to dry. Herbs were the favorite of the 'wise woman' as she knew the medicinal value of each and every plant. She also knew that picking flowers or herbs at night actually does improve the potency of the herbs chemical healing value. She certainly was truly a practitioner of a Nature at best. She also was well aware that what we take from nature, we must return in kind to maintain the balance and equilibrium. The modern man has, however, forgotten this and has paid the price in form of many ecological and environmental disasters. However, with the New Age movement, many people have started reintroducing Witchcraft as the true religion of God and Nature. There is renewed interest in Witchcraft, Wicca and Witches profess to believe and practice their craft with a sense of pride and confidence. But one must ask, with all this ancient wisdom awakening, why are things such a mess? Something is missing!

BIOGRAPHY:

UR-ADORABELLE always had a deep fascination with nature throughout her life. She grew up in a semirural part of New England. Being the eldest of 4 children, and having a mentally unstable mother, she was given the task of being 'in charge' and had more than her share of responsibility for their welfare most of her childhood. They all loved to explore nature with her as it was one of her greatest passions. Even though she grew up a faithful Catholic, she now recognizes the fact that in her youth, that the forest was her church. Nature was her go to for peace and bliss. She seemed to have the uncanny ability to communicate with the land and many of its little creatures.

During her teen years, her parents divorced, and she found herself drifting away from her true love – nature. For many years, Ur-Adorabelle work in retail but eventually found that it did not serve her life purpose. So, in her forties, she went back to school to become a massage therapist. Several years following, after studying Druidism, she found her way back to nature.

Although she never saw herself as a writer, she became inspired to write during her first year of the druid training. Her urgent concern for the environment's welfare has directed her down the path of inspiring others to follow suit.

Acknowledgments:

First, I'd like to acknowledge ALL my teachers – the ones that led me down the path of enlightenment and those who showed me paths that weren't for my best and highest good. Thank you!

Without ado, I'm conveying much love and gratitude to my Guides, Angels, Ancestors, Masters and the Divine. Thanks for gently guiding me and sometimes pushing me to achieve my best!

I'm sending a big etheric love hug to one of my favorite mentors and best friend who happened to be my beloved brother, David. One of his many gifts was having the knack for bringing out the best in those he encountered. He exuded unconditional love to everyone and set a remarkable example of treating everyone with dignity and grace – naturally. He certainly was an enlightened soul and also had a passion for writing. David passed to the other side in 1987. However, I always feel his presence when I think of him.

I appreciate the support from my darling sisters, Jackie and Annie who've always shown admiration towards my creativity. Much love to them all.

I honor my Druid teachers from the Green Mountain Druid Order – Fearn Lickfield and her husband, the late Ivan McBeth. In 2010, I was without a doubt, Divinely guided to their teachings. Fearn and Ivan inspired me to re-connect to my first love – Nature! For years I was searching and searching for my lost purpose and passion until I rooted myself into the Druid training. For me, it was life changing. Ivan re-introduced me to the energy of dragon and that energy has never left my side.

In November of 2016, the inspiration for my book came directly from watching the brave and 'peaceful warriors' at Standing Rock. The Indigenous Natives from the West showed me that courage and tenacity is what makes a person stand up for what they believe in. They might have not won that fight however they did win my heart. So, my heart goes out to ALL Indigenous Peoples throughout the world who are courageous and connected so deeply to the love of their Ancestors, Nature and Mother Earth. They showed me that unity and community is what makes a village work successfully on both a physical and soul level. I believe that the Indigenous peoples are the wisdom keepers of Mother Earth. Their faithfulness in the spirit of the land is priceless. They showed me to never ever give up. I'm dedicating this book to ALL Indigenous Peoples!

Be Aware of the Dragon

by Adora Belle Fleur, Druid of the GMDO written on 10-17-14

Woken to the watchful eye
Bright gold and rich with wisdom
Who are you I asked?
'I am the Master of Chi
Known to you as Dragon'

How come I've not seen you here before?
'I live in the lower world'
What do you do there?
'I help the elements transform Chi'
Curious how is that so?
'I arise from the bowels of earth
With ground shaking tremors
Freeing fiery volcanic frenzies
Triggering massive tidal waves of emotion
And initiating storms that demand change'

Can you help people?
'Of course,
for eons the Asians have known my secret'
Interesting how so?
'Master Chi with Martial Arts and I'll help you'
What class do you recommend?
'Qi Gong'
Just wondering how often?
'Continuously'

*With gratitude
I am now aware of the Dragon
And its secret lives within me!*